MW01251811

IN THE SUMMER OF 1941, shipbuilder Joe Felice answers the call to join the war effort. He volunteers as an air raid warden in the newly created Office of Civilian Defense. Joe and his buddies patrol the streets of Dory Harbor, Massachusetts, during the mandated blackouts.

AT THE END OF A MIDNIGHT shift, Joe follows a sliver of light from inside the local barber shop, intending to issue a citation to the violator. Instead, he stumbles across the body of his friend and fellow warden, Frank Costello. Desperate to get justice for Frank, and clear his name, Joe persuades his college-student daughter to help him investigate.

BLACKOUT '41

Camille Minichino

ISBN: 9798859101818

*Cover and Book Design:
Brian Shea*
CROW & QUOIN BOOKS

Dory Harbor, Massachusetts

August, 1941

FORTY-THREE-YEAR-OLD Joe Felice slid into one of the chairs meant for second graders at the Abraham Lincoln Grammar School. The large brick building was empty except for the classroom dedicated to training Civil Defense volunteers.

Joe looked around the room and felt sorry for the guys who weren't as small and fit as he was. He knew most of the men, like the street-corner bookies Petey O and

Salvie Sausage, each of whom probably weighed twice what he did. They had to be hurting as the desks that were attached to the chairs dug into their pot bellies.

The group had assembled for a meeting of local air raid wardens. Joe was glad he'd dressed up for tonight's special meeting, a one-on-one interview with their trainer. The final step in their official certification. It was like school in a way, and he wanted to take it seriously this time.

They'd all been patrolling the streets of Dory Harbor, Massachusetts, for a few weeks. "Probation" it was called, as if they'd just gotten released from a stint on Deer Island. The men were sticklers. God help anyone who kept a light on during a mandatory blackout or wandered outside after curfew. These guys in helmets and arm bands would be on the offender with

a writeup and a fine before you could say
Uncle Sam.

"You're all decked out, like a three-
star general," Joe's daughter, Marie had
said, straightening his tie. earlier that evening.

He knew he'd never look as sharp as
Frank Costello. Poor Frank, though, with a
name that matched one of big crime bosses. Frankie didn't seem to mind the teas-
ing, as long as it came from a *compare* and
not some *stunato*. Frankie and the rest of
the guys had very little to do all day except
hang around in their nice slacks and shirts,
take bets, or visit a rations customer over a
cup of "coffee and." Joe smiled at "and,"
which meant whatever booze the house-
hold could spare to top off the coffee.

Now in the classroom, Guido, who
was always in trouble, sent a spitball

Joe's way.

"Heads up, Happy Joe," Guido said. "See what you missed not going to second grade?" He got a straw ready for another shot.

"Leave Joe alone," Petey O said, grinning. "Pick on someone your own size."

"*Afanabala*," Salvie said, and hit Petey O.

"No swearing, Salvie," Joe said. "We're in a school. And what if Mr. C comes in?"

"No problem," Salvie said. "That Irishman won't know what we're saying anyway."

"That don't make it right," Joe slipped out of his chair, gathered the spitballs that had accumulated, and tossed them in the wastebasket at the front of the room.

The guys laughed at him, but he knew

it was all in fun. These were his friends, *paesani* who knew he was a hard-working laborer. Joe was less flush than they were, and they often let him win at poker.

Still, Joe wished they'd behave. What if their trainer came in and caught them goofing off? He might cancel the session and fire every one of them. It wasn't the first time his pals acted up while they were waiting for Mr. Callahan. Sometimes Joe felt like standing up and making a speech, like the ones President Roosevelt gave on the radio.

"Take your patriotism seriously," he'd say.

Frank Costello, Joe's partner on all his blackout shifts, was the biggest clothes horse of them all, and he loved to talk about his duds and how he could beat rationing through his connections. Frank was quiet about his outfit today however, though he had on a new summer jacket. He was jumpy, tapping his foot really fast, as if he had to be somewhere soon.

The best Joe could do to spruce up was dig the dirt from under his fingernails, but he was satisfied. Marie had taken the time to buy him a special cream he could use to slick down his hair. He was proud of his daughter, studying to be a lawyer at a college in Boston. She'd worked hard enough at her uncle's pizza concession on the beach to be able spend a term in the dorms. He missed her cooking, so much like her late mother's. Joe refused to roll up his sleeves and ruin the nice ironing job Marie had done though the classroom was hot and stuffy.

Marie had practiced with him and told him not to worry. Mostly, Marie knew how to make him relax. She made him feel smart that he knew how to do so many things. Electrical, plumbing, carpentry, painting, even though he wasn't aces at any one thing.

"A little of this and a little of that," she'd said, twisting her wrist at the same time. "Right?" And they'd both cracked up.

At under five feet—only by half an inch, he claimed—Joe was the shortest guy in the Civil Defense crew, too short to be drafted. But he made up for it in enthusiasm.

Joe wanted more than anything to do his part for the war effort. He was thrilled at this chance to help out at home. He had his own way of catching up with the news from the front. He wasn't much for reading, not like Marie. He could read the headlines, though, and sat riveted during the movie theater newsreels where you could watch explosions at sea and attacks on aircraft firsthand. His jaw tensed at the sight of bombed-out cities across the ocean. He knew he had to keep that from happening in America.

He'd easily passed the training exercises, memorizing all the routes, where the call boxes into the police station were, even first aid instructions. But he was worried about today's interview. It didn't help that he now sat in a real classroom, surrounded by reminders of his lack of education. Besides the framed photo of Abraham Lincoln—Principal De Marco had called him the patron saint of the school—the walls were covered with samples of geography and history and arithmetic. Plus, the war overseas. Joe's eyes were drawn to a set of posters. He squinted, as if that would help him figure out the words. He could read the easy ones. DON'T WASTE FOOD and SAVE GUM FOIL. Another poster had words he couldn't read, but from the picture of an explosion and rows of burned-out houses, he got the point.

He admired the guys in the room who didn't seem at all worried about facing Mr. C one to one. In fact, they acted like the second graders whose seats they filled, with paper airplanes and more spitballs flying across the air. The heftiest of them, Guido, was at the blackboard using what looked like brand-new chalk to draw a picture of a naked lady.

"Is that your *goomah*?" Frank asked.

"Just because you have a few," Petey O said, sparking more dirty talk.

Joe tuned out. He thought about his hero, the president, and his regular "fireside chats" on the radio. FDR had kept his promise to increase the shipbuilding industry, and now Joe had the best job of his life, in an emergency shipyard. The new ships were small and uncomplicated and could be turned out quickly by simple labor and carpentry, ready to carry cargo wherever it was needed. Joe didn't mind when the President called these fast-turn-around ships "the ugly ducklings of the fleet."

Mr. Callahan entered the classroom, and all the guys shuffled their feet under their desks and straightened their shoulders. Guido had barely finished erasing his nude-girly sketch before Mr. C strode in.

Their trainer stood facing the American Flag that hung from a pole attached to a corner of the room. The men wrestled their way out of the chairs, Guido almost taking his with him as he made his way to upright.

The men all managed to remain straight-faced during the Pledge of Allegiance, but afterwards, Petey O whispered, "Play ball."

Joe rolled his eyes.

"Felice, Joseph A.," Mr. C boomed, sending a slight shiver through Joe's body. What if Mr. C thought it was Joe who'd said, "Play ball?"

Petey O reached over, nearly tipping over the desk-chair combo. He nudged Joe. "He's calling you, Happy Joe. You'll do fine. Warm him up for us."

Joe gulped. He remembered all the practice time Marie had spent with him, and the knot in his stomach loosened.

Salvie chuckled. "Yeah, warm him up. And if you don't know the answer, make it up."

"I will," Joe whispered. "I'll give him a little of this and a little of that."

"CAN YOU USE a gun?" Mr. C asked.

Joe shook his head. "No."

"How about a gas mask. Ever use one?"

"No."

After a few more "no's", Mr. C laughed. "What's the best attribute you bring to this job, Joe?"

Att-ri-bute? Marie had taught him that whenever he didn't know a word someone used, to think about the whole sentence and make a good guess. He knew what "best" meant, so he gave it a shot.

"I can run up a flight of steps really fast without getting winded."

"Okay." Mr. C smiled and scratched behind his ear.

"And I can crawl into very small spaces."

"I suppose that might come in handy."

Joe nodded. "One time I rescued my daughter's friend's cat from a crawl space under their house."

Mr. C laughed this time.

Joe didn't know whether that was good or bad, but he continued. "The poor thing was trapped in a cross fitting."

"In a what?"

Joe made a cross with his two index fingers. "You know, a pipe fitting, like the push fit you have sometimes. One of the cat's paws was stuck in—"

Mr. C stood up and held out his hand. "Congratulations, Joe."

JOE LOOKED FORWARD to his shifts with Frank as his partner, six to midnight, three nights a week, and he was the first one to raise his hand if a substitute was needed any other night. He loved hanging his whistle around his neck, strapping on his helmet. His arm band was decorated with a dark blue circle patch and thick red stripes. Mr. C explained that the stripes stood for the many duties an air raid warden had, besides checking for lights. Like directing people to a shelter if needed or reporting any gas smells. Not quite a soldier's duties, but close enough to make Joe feel he was doing his part.

This Friday evening, Joe headed for the Civil Defense Office, a suite of rooms in the Dory Harbor City Hall, a brick building at least one hundred years old. An important officer from Washington DC the men seldom saw, sat in the innermost office. In the outer office Petey O's wife, Nettie, kept track of schedules, personnel, patrol routes, and any other CD-related clerical matters.

Joe climbed the marble steps, so old they were worn in the middle, to the second floor to check in with Nettie. Her office was small enough that the desk fan, set on a file cabinet, made for a pleasant breeze.

He opened the door to find Nettie high on a ladder hammering away at what looked like a new bulletin board.

"They wanted me to wait for maintenance to come and mount this, but I'm not about to wait till Christmas," she shouted down to Joe.

"How did you get that heavy thing up there?"

Nettie put the hammer on the ladder's shelf. She flexed the muscle of her right arm. "See this? It's what you get from waitressing for fifteen years before this cushy job came along." She gave the bulletin board's frame one last whack before descending to her desk.

"I baked some cookies for you," Nettie said, reaching into the bottom drawer. She pulled out a package wrapped in waxed paper, labeled "JF." Joe noticed others, as usual, labeled with familiar initials, for Frank and Tony, and other guys who weren't married.

Joe pressed the package to his chest. "The next time Marie has a chance to bake, I'm going to bring you some for a change."

Nettie waved away the idea. "Don't worry about that. I'm trying to put some meat on your bones. Marie's, too. She's very pretty, Joe, but she could use a few pounds. I told Petey we need to bring a pot of gravy by your place this week-end. Don't tell him I said so"—Nettie switched to a whisper though no one else was around—"but Petey could do with less meat."

Joe kept his agreement to himself, mentally comparing Petey's spare tire around his waist with his wife's impressive biceps.

Nettie handed Joe a schedule, a neatly typed carbon paper copy. He searched for his name and let out a gasp.

His eyes widened. "I'm alone tonight?"

"Yeah, Frank was supposed to call you. He had some business to take care of and couldn't get out of it. He didn't call you?"

Joe shook his head. He felt his chest tighten.

The men were usually paired up, and

Joe liked it that way. Even after more than a month, he lacked confidence. His handwriting wasn't that great, his spelling even worse. When an incident called for writing up a ticket, he counted on passing it off to his partner.

"You're a pro by now," Nettie said.

Joe fiddled as usual with Nettie's ashtray, a fancy brass globe. He slid the ring past the equator, and the earth opened up to reveal lipstick-stained butts.

"I guess so," Joe said, closing the earth again. "It's just for tonight, right?"

"Yeah, and look, Joe"—Nettie turned a bit to face the large map of the town on the wall behind her— "your route is in your own neighborhood. Between Malden and Prospect Streets. You won't have a problem."

Joe wasn't so sure, but he didn't want

to call Nettie a liar. "Yeah, that's right," he said. He grabbed the package of cookies and left the office.

Tonight would be a real test, working alone. He did know how to use the call boxes on his route, he reminded himself, so he could always call the cop manning the station if he needed help.

As soon as he got to the stairway to leave City Hall, he moved Nettie's cookies to his left hand and made the sign of the cross with his right. He pictured the big statue of Saint Anthony in front of his church a few blocks away.

Please no trouble tonight.

SO FAR SO GOOD.

Patrolling alone hadn't been too bad,

23

and his replacements would be showing up in less than an hour. The only hitch had been when he'd needed to make a call to report on Billy Cannella, a teenager who lived in the neighborhood. He'd had to haul Billy with him to the nearest call box, use his key to access the phone and talk to the cop on duty, while at the same time holding onto the offending young citizen.

Billy had broken curfew to visit his girlfriend, and Joe'd caught him. Then the kid got mad at Joe and refused to help him out with the spelling of community when Joe wanted to write "community service" on his report.

"You can't arrest me," Billy taunted.

"Don't be so sure about that," Joe said. The words of Mr. Callahan, rang in his ears and he repeated them to Billy:

An air raid warden is not a doctor, or

a cop, or a fireman, but he may be called on to perform any of these duties.

"Never mind," Billy said. He slipped his arm from Joe's grasp and ran toward home.

Joe called after him. "The cops already know what you did. I told them on the phone."

Billy turned just long enough to thumb his nose at Joe.

Could have been worse. Joe shook his head. Billy was no longer his problem.

Other than that bratty teenager, Joe had met no other resisters, nor had he seen any lights that might alert an enemy plane to a target on the ground.

He thought of the news he listened to on the radio and the newspaper reports Marie read to him. He listened intently to what was going on in Europe, from men like Edward R. Murrow and Eric Sevareid. Sometimes when he was listening to them on the radio, he could hear the sirens in the background in another country overseas.

Everyone seemed to agree: this war would be fought in the air, which made Joe's air raid warden job all the more important.

JOE CHECKED THE barely visible clock in the window of the Dory Harbor Repair shop. Twenty past eleven, and still warm and muggy. Joe was tempted to remove his helmet but instead mopped under the heavy hat with his handkerchief. He knew that once in a while an official from the state would drive by and make sure things were running smoothly in the county. Joe didn't want to be caught bareheaded if that guy chose tonight to check on his patrol.

He took a quick break on a bus stop bench and ate a few of Nettie's cookies. He left a couple for Marie, who came home every other weekend. He didn't know what he'd do without his daughter. He wished he could provide her with nice things. It wasn't fair that she had an unskilled worker for a father. He thought of the nylon stockings Frank and Salvie Sausage and the other guys brought their wives and girlfriends when they returned from trips to Connecticut or New Hampshire. The black market was thriving and Joe couldn't afford to take advantage of it.

Joe walked the rest of his shift along Prospect, which had mostly single-family homes, all in total darkness. He circled back to Malden, his own street of apartment buildings, then crossed over to inspect his building. He started at the top, squinting a bit, clearing the fourth, then the third floor, then his floor, directly above Tony's Barber Shop.

One more level, the street level, where Tony's was closed and dark for the night. All was well. That was it. For all practical purposes, Joe's shift was over. Less than a half hour and he'd be done. He plopped down on the curb and waited for Petey O and Salvie Sausage to show up to replace him.

He couldn't wait to take his helmet off. Plus, the arm band and long-sleeved shirt seemed to have tightened on his body since tonight's blackout started.

He bent over to loosen the lacings on his shoes. His socks were damp with sweat. As usual, one full tub of lukewarm water was what he needed. The sooner, the better.

He adjusted his lacings and raised his head to sit back up.

And saw a sliver of light from the bottom edge of Tony's door.

No. He couldn't tell if he'd said it out loud. No. He slid down, sprawled on his side on the sidewalk. No mistake. A light. No!

This time, he knew he'd yelled it.

He was going to have to cross the street again, peer into the shop's window, and knock on the door until he got the attention of whoever was inside. Tony? Charlie, Tony's assistant? Buster, the kid who swept up the place? Or maybe one of them had left a light on by mistake and no one was in the shop now. No matter what, Joe would have to run to the call box around the corner and let the night crew at the station know what was going on as soon as he figured it out. He'd have to write up a report, too, but he hoped his friends in the next crew might show up in time to help him with that.

Joe made his way across the street. Halfway there, he saw a figure push open the front door, rush down the two steps to the sidewalk, and make a beeline up Malden Street. Too dark to tell who it was, except he was sure Tony couldn't run that fast. Not Charlie either. Buster, maybe.

He had a choice. Chase the guy running away or go into the shop and turn off the light. If it was a light. Now he wasn't sure. His eyes seemed to be failing him when he really needed them. He made a quick decision. Check the inside of the shop first, and make sure there's no light on. The safety and protection of the country came first. Later, he'd write up the curfew violator who'd left the light on, and mention that he didn't get a look at the guy. Maybe he'd been after Tony's special lotion. What else had any value? A bunch of combs Tony kept in a drawer? Towels? He knew Tony emptied the cash out every day.

Joe hurried through the door of the shop. He spotted the source of the light. An angle-head flashlight on the floor near one of barber chairs. He picked it up, trying to switch it off at the same time. But before he could manipulate the switch, the beam fell on the back of a head.

Someone was sitting in the black leather chair.

Someone not moving.

His partner, Frank Costello, with a nylon stocking wrapped tight around his neck.

JOE WAS STILL a little shaky. Before he knew it, the intersection between Malden Street and Broadway was like a zoo. The Dory Harbor phone lines must have been all lit up, the story flying, because a big crowd came out to see what was happening. It was still pitch black, but so loud Joe thought a Messerschmitt could have found them, no problem, by following the sound.

The weather held fast as warm and muggy and now Joe sat on the curb again, the spot where he'd first noticed the sliver of light. He figured it came from the flashlight that Frank or the guy who killed him dropped. He hoped Frank had given him what-for at least.

He wished he'd chased the guy instead of going into the shop. Frank was dead.

He wasn't going anywhere. But if that was the guy who'd killed Frank, well, would he have given a second thought to killing Joe, too?

A lot of Joe's buddies came over to the curb to talk to him.

"How you doing?" they wanted to know. Petey O, Salvie, Guido, all of them, their wives and girlfriends.

Joe didn't know how he was doing.

It wasn't like he'd never seen a dead body. A few years ago, he'd done a stint as a janitor at Della Russo's Funeral Home, the mortuary preferred by the members of Saint Anthony's Parish. At first, Joe was supposed to clean only the areas used by the public, but he'd taken overtime whenever they offered it and more than once he found himself alone at night with a body—a client, was what Al Della Russo called the dead people.

And there was Rose, too—Joe made the sign of the cross, kissed his thumb and index finger—Marie's mother. He didn't want to think of those days.

Besides, it was different tonight. Frank hadn't died peacefully in the arms of a wife or a girlfriend, or in a hospital bed with a caring nurse. He had been strangled to death in their friend Tony's barber shop.

Joe raised his head for a minute, searching the crowd for Tony but couldn't find him. The police had already strung rope across the entrance of the shop. The ambulance parked in front blocked Joe's view, and three police cars in the small area didn't help. He went back to slumping over, his elbows on his knees, his head down.

He couldn't erase the image. How Frank's eyes were wide open, bulging, blood pooling in the corners. There were scratch marks on Frank's cheeks. He must have fought to get free of the stocking. It had fallen away a little and before he'd killed the flashlight Joe could see bruises on Frank's cheek.

Joe took a breath. Waves of guilt washed over him. He could have kicked himself that he'd been angry with Frank for copping out of his patrol duty tonight. If he'd only known. He'd been quick to judge, that Frank had gone off to collect on a debt or gin up a new customer for his black-market inventory. But maybe if his buddy had come for his shift, he wouldn't be dead now? Either way, it was too much to take in.

A young cop on the scene found Joe. "You were supposed to wait by the call box," he said.

Joe stood up, banged his forehead with the palm of his hand. All that training for what to do in an emergency and when a real crisis came along, he'd failed.

"I forgot," he said. "I'm sorry." Joe's voice was hoarse, as if he were on the edge of tears.

The cop put his hand on Joe's shoulder. "Okay. That's all right."

"Can I go home now?" Joe asked. At least he'd remembered he couldn't leave without permission.

"I'm afraid you're going to have to wait until one of the detectives comes over. He should be ready for you any minute."

Joe pointed to his building. "I live right there." Joe had in mind inviting the detectives up for coffee. He could turn on the fan for them. Share Nettie's cookies.

"You live above the crime scene?" the

cop asked.

Officer Donovan he called himself, made it sound as though Joe had killed his friend, just because he lived so close.

"I'm a volunteer air raid warden." Joe showed him the Civil Defense patch on his sleeve. "I was at the end of my shift, ready to go upstairs to my flat, when I saw the light under the door to the barber shop. I'm supposed to go in and check whenever I see a light."

Officer Donovan held up his hand in a "stop" signal. "Sir, it's better that you save your comments for the detectives. They'll know what questions to ask. They'll take notes, too. It's better all-around if you wait for them. Okay with you, Sir?"

Joe nodded. "Okay."

Joe couldn't remember anyone calling him "Sir," let alone twice. He hadn't had much experience with cops, except for the men who came around to talk to the volunteers during training sessions at the school. They'd all seemed very friendly and even wrote the number of the direct line to the station on the blackboard, in case anyone had questions later.

Joe sat down to wait on the curb again as the ambulance took Frank away. Finally, he saw shiny shoes planted in front of him. He stood up quickly.

"Mr. Felice? I'm Detective O'Fallon." The tall skinny redhead looked young enough to be Joe's son. "I'd like to ask you a few questions. Why don't you come down to the station with me?"

It didn't sound like a question.

THE LAST TIME JOE was in the Dory Harbor police station had been for a special lecture to the air raid wardens on the state of the war around the globe. Joe learned about leaders he was not familiar with, except in newsreels, places he'd never been. The British and Australians in North Africa. Benghazi captured. Yugoslavia surrendering. Mussolini. Rommel. Forty thousand civilians killed in London alone.

The police chief himself had addressed the men that evening, treating them like valued soldiers, encouraging them to continue performing their important duties. They were true patriots, he'd told them. A long table held a coffee service and enough doughnuts for a real army.

That wasn't so long ago, and now here he was in the same building, in the same lobby checking in with the same sergeant, only this time he'd been made to walk between two officers. He'd seen all his friends talking to the detective tonight like he was. Had any of the others been brought to the station, too? Petey O? Tony? Salvie? Guido?

If so, they weren't in the same lobby. Joe'd been brought to a marked up wooden bench, an officer stationed in front of him, as if Joe were ready to bolt.

"Later," the officer said when he asked to call Marie.

On the bench next to his was a sad-looking guy, curled up, snoring loudly, looking as comfortable as if he were in a first-class hotel.

More than once, Joe tried to tell a passing cop or detective that he had nothing to do with what happened to Frank, in case that's why they'd taken him here. He'd

seen a light and gone to check. That was
what his training taught him to do. Track it
down. Snuff it out. Report it.

Joe had lost track of time. And he'd
forgotten to wind his watch. He strained
to read a clock far down a hallway. Two
o'clock, maybe.

Detective O'Fallon came back. Don't
cops ever go home? "You can call your
lawyer now," he told Joe.

"I don't have a lawyer. I don't need
one."

"Everyone needs a lawyer."

"I want to call my daughter. She's in
college in Boston. She's studying to—."

"Come with me," O'Fallon said.

He didn't want to worry Marie, but
he didn't want her to find out about Frank
some other way. The detective accompa-
nied Joe to the phone and motioned for an

officer to take his place behind Joe. The phone hung on the wall, with no dividers or anything to make a private call.

Marie had given him the number for the phone in the hallway on her dorm floor and Joe gave it to the operator now. Eventually, a young woman's voice, not Marie's, answered.

"Fitzgerald Hall."

"I'm sorry to wake you up, but can you find Marie Felice for me? This is not her weekend to come home, but I'm her father and I need to talk to her real bad."

"Oh, sure. She's in the reading room. I'll get her."

Joe had no idea what a reading room would look like but knowing his daughter, that was where she would be. And at two in the morning.

"Pa, what is it?"

Joe blew out a long breath. He knew he'd never be able to forget the image of his friend sitting in the barber chair, as the two of them had done so many times over the years. He knew he had to keep it together as he told his daughter what happened, from finding the body of the man she called her Uncle Frank to where he was calling from, surrounded by police.

When they both could breathe somewhat normally, Marie asked questions as if she were already a lawyer.

"When was the last time you saw Uncle Frank?"

At poker on Thursday night.

"Did he seem upset about anything?"

Nothing unusual.

"As far as you know, was he in debt? Did he owe anyone a lot of money?"

I don't think so. He always had a lot

43

of cash on him.

"Like all my other uncles?"

"Like all your other uncles."

"Anything in his personal life?"

"You mean with his new friend?"

Joe smiled in spite of his grief. He thought of Frank's girlfriends, as well as those some of his married buddies had on the side. Sometimes the girls even came to poker night, careful to check who else might be present. Something Joe would never understand, but he was determined not to judge them.

"As far as you know, was Uncle Frank involved in anything illegal?"

"Uh."

"Okay, never mind. You're standing out in the open at the police station, aren't you?"

"That's right, *Carissima.*"

"Hold on, Pa."

While Marie was silent, Joe tried to read some of the messages scribbled on the wall around the phone. He saw hearts with initials in them, but mostly pretty bad words.

Marie came back on the line just as the officer was about to take the phone from Joe.

"I'm coming home, Pa," she said. "My roommate said her boyfriend can drive me. There won't be any traffic at this hour."

Joe felt immediate relief. "If you're sure."

"Of course. Can you put the detective on the line with me? I have an idea. I think I know how to find out who killed Uncle Frank."

JOE LOST HIS BATTLE to get the cop assigned to him to let him go home. Marie would think he was home, he said.

"So what?" the cop said. "She's a smart college kid, right? She'll figure it out."

"She'll be hungry."

The cop laughed. "There's a vending machine down the hall."

And so on.

The cop had been right. Marie found her father on the lobby bench. At least Joe had convinced the cop-guard not to handcuff him. He couldn't bear to have his daughter see him that way.

True to her word, Marie had a plan for flushing out her Uncle Frank's killer. Joe couldn't have been prouder of his daughter as she managed to get a meeting with Detective O'Fallon. She explained her plan and he agreed to give it a try.

THE NEXT EVENING, Joe sat with the gang in the back room of De Maino's Pizza Parlor for a regular game of poker. The group included some of the women and Marie, who was treated like a special guest.

"I needed to be near my Uncle Frank's family and friends during this sad time," she'd said.

The players had decided Frank would want them to carry on and that whoever won would take the whole pot to Lucia, Frank's mother, to show their support.

Halfway through five-card draw, Joe knew it was time to carry out his part in Marie's plan. He had so much faith in her, he was hardly nervous. Besides, he could look across the table at her and know she'd rescue him if he made a mistake.

"Oh, by the way," he said as casually as possible. "There's a little good news. The detective who's been grilling me told me they got a tip about the guy who killed Frank. I guess he dropped something in the shop as he ran out. That's why they're leaving the rope around the doorway, so they can search for it tomorrow morning."

Cheers all around.

"What is it?" Tony asked. "What did the guy leave behind?"

Joe shrugged. "He wouldn't say. Just that it was something that for sure pointed to the killer."

"Why do they have to wait till tomorrow? Why can't they go right now?" Petey O asked.

Marie was ready for this. "They're short-handed here on the weekend, and apparently some of the crew was called away to help with a big robbery in Chelsea."

"And it's not going anywhere, whatever the thing is," Joe said, glad to add his bit.

"This is great news," Clara, Salvie's wife, said. "I keep thinking, what if the guy's running around looking for another one of us to kill?"

Joe let out a long breath and said no one was more relieved than he was. And they continued the game.

SUNDAY, AND THERE WAS nothing more to do but wait. The game had ended about one in the morning, and Joe and Marie knew that by two o'clock every guy in the group, their wives, girlfriends, bookies, bookies' bosses and black-market suppliers and customers would know of the planted tip.

Detective O'Fallon insisted that only his team would be in attendance on the stakeout in the darkened barber shop. Joe and Marie were to go to the Police Station and wait there. If the plan worked and Frank's killer took the bait, they'd see the culprit towed in, in handcuffs.

It seemed to take forever as Joe and Marie ate whatever you called a middle-of-the-night meal in one of the station's interview rooms. Joe hadn't wanted to eat much since the sirens had taken over his street on Friday night, but when Marie opened the bag with his favorite sandwich, he was ready to dig in. The three P's he called it. Prosciutto, provolone, and peppers. It smelled so good, Marie had to promise to bring one for each of the officers in the station before she went back to school.

When they finished eating, Joe and Marie walked out of the room and sat on a bench in the lobby.

Just in time to see the front door open and the detective and two policemen walk in with Frank's killer in handcuffs.

Petey O's wife, Nettie, spoke in a loud voice as she passed their bench. "After all the sneaking around, delivering his stolen goods, and everything else I did for Frank, in and out of bed. Can you believe, the stockings were not for me?"

— **Selected Novels** —

Writing as CAMILLE MINICHINO:

The Periodic Table Mysteries
   The Hydrogen Murder
   The Helium Murder
   The Lithium Murder
   The Beryllium Murder
   The Boric Acid Murder
   The Carbon Murder
   The Nitrogen Murder
   The Oxygen Murder

The Miniature Mysteries
   Murder in Miniature
   Mayhem in Miniature
   Malice in Miniature
   Mourning in Miniature
   Monster in Miniature
   Mix-up in Miniature
   Madness in Miniature

Writing as ELIZABETH LOGAN:

The Alaska Diner Mysteries
Moose and Murder
Fishing for Trouble
Murphy's Slaw

NONFICTION

How to Live with an Engineer *(Amazon)*
Essays in *Mystery Readers Journal*

STORIES IN ANTHOLOGIES

Happy Homicides vols 1 and 2
Sleuthing Women vol 2
Midcentury Murder
Low Down Dirty Vote vols 1, 2, and 3